CRICKET PUBLISHING / U.S.A.

Copyright © 2018 by Mandy Jackson-Beverly

All rights reserved. Published by Cricket
Publishing, established 2015.

Jackson-Beverly, Mandy.
The Legend of Astridr: Birth / by Mandy
Jackson-Beverly. — 1st ed.
https://mandyjacksonbeverly.com

Library of Congress Control Number: 2018908029
Hardcover ISBN: 978-0-9965088-7-2
E-Book ISBN: 978-0-9965088-6-5
Paperback ISBN: 978-09965088-8-9

Cover Design: Damonza
Formatting: Damonza

THE
LEGEND *of* ASTRIDR

BIRTH

ILLUSTRATIONS *by*
+ BECKY STONEHOUSE +

+ MANDY JACKSON-BEVERLY +

RELATIONSHIPS

The story of Astridr begins not with her birth, or even her youth, but rather with the story of her ancestors, for although we are born to explore our own path, we are also linked to our history, woven from a thin thread connecting us to our forefathers. Every decision, every love-filled moment, every fear and net of deceit thrown around us, all are reflections of the shadows of our memories and are derived from our paternal and maternal collective. Our cells hold the consciousness of our past encounters, and it is our choice whether to learn from them and find peace or lie stagnant and wither.

But as necessary as our blood relatives are, so are the friends and adoptive family members we meet, for they are our teachers just as we are theirs. Such is the case in The Legend of Astridr; for the immortal who once protected a mother would later become her daughter's eternal friend and confidante. And although the friends' journeys move along separate paths—one, a protector of the arts; the other, a warrior—their calls to each other reach beyond any measure of space.

CHAPTER 1

GUNWALD AND SKULD

N THE FAR north where the earth moved in torpid time, a woman dressed in a cloak of pearl-colored velvet halted in her steps. Light glistened on her skin, making it appear like translucent alabaster, and the ivory white of her irises was framed with a background of ice-flowing water. She scanned the vast plateau where snowflakes fallen over past millennia now rested, deep under a slab of thick ice—a steadily moving form that shaped the valley of the windswept tundra sleeping in a cradle of jagged, snow-covered mountains. The landscape was a quiet place where science collided with nature to create visions of supreme beauty, a slumber of sweet innocence.

The woman was recognizable as the Lady and the Rose, but that was not always her name. Before the first falling known as Ragnarök, three women lived in the Well of Urd, the first root of the sacred ash tree, Yggdrasil. These three demigoddesses, or Norns as they were known, shaped the destiny of all beings. The Norn named Skuld—meaning future—was rescued from the falling ash tree by the fae king Gunwald. Skuld and Gunwald had been in love for many years and were now free to roam together above the roots of Yggdrasil and enter the world of mortals.

Their love brought them a son, a fae prince whose destiny would bring him responsibilities that, like they had his father, would at times pull him away from his beloved. For the fates of the immortal are tethered to the well-being of the mother of this earth. But mirroring the cycle of birth, death, and rebirth was the path of Skuld. Although her sisters were long gone, as the lone survivor she carried the weight of the Well of Urd—the Well of Destiny—in her blood.

Throughout her life, Skuld had experienced a recurring vision where she stood in a garden of roses. Each time she entered the dream, the petals on the roses were fewer until the ground beneath her lay covered in hues of pink and red, leaving the bushes bare, their limbs naked except for an armor of deadly thorns. Skuld picked up a handful of petals and watched as they ascended, forming a trail upward to the heavens, only to rain upon the earth in a deluge of crimson-tinged hail. All around her, the ground was covered in blood-splattered pages from books, mutilated paintings, damaged musical instruments, and torn dancing slippers. Skuld knew the occurrence to be divine—a message from the ancient ones that she should protect the beauty of the arts.

In another vision, Skuld saw a woman with eyes that sparkled gold and hair white—like freshly fallen snow that long ago fell on the lost lands of Niflheim. But Skuld also saw a dark cloud hovering above the woman, threatening to end the cycles of the earth mother and push all life toward the cycle of death, toward the second Ragnarök.

Later that day, Gunwald found Skuld in the Forest of the Dryads, sobbing onto a bed of rose petals. She told him of her visions, and as she did her tears turned pink and roses lifted from the ground and twirled until they formed a curtain around the two lovers. Gunwald took his beloved to the plane of endless love and pure tranquility on a bed of sweet-smelling petals, and in the tender moments that linger after passion, Skuld shared with him what she had seen and the identity of the beautiful young woman who roamed the earth as a savior of the creative essence. She was their granddaughter.

But as with all love, Gunwald and Skuld's relationship was not without heartache. One day while the two lovers were crossing the tundra, Gunwald's heart was pierced with a silver arrow tainted with Charon's obol. As he lay dying, Freyja appeared, ready to carry the fae king to the depths of her world.

"Please, no!" And as Skuld fell across her beloved's dying body, the vast glaciers began to melt and everything around her started to wane.

"Stop!" yelled Freyja. "This world must not die, Skuld. Cease your tears."

Skuld lifted her head slowly and stared up at Freyja. "You ask too much, for my heart is breaking."

Freyja knelt next to Skuld. "He cannot live here on this plane."

"Then let him live in another," Skuld said. "We have seen our son's daughter—she will be more powerful than I. If you take Gunwald to your world, our granddaughter's life will not be, for if Gunwald dies, our son will not have a purpose, nor will I."

Freyja gazed around at the dying world. "I can take him below this place," she said. "Gunwald will live, and you can use your magic to speak with him."

Skuld closed her eyes and screamed her son's name. "Hakon!"

In a flash, her son stood beside her and took his father's hand in his own. "Who did this? Who would tarnish a silver arrow with such a thing as the boatman's coin?" He glared with fury at Freyja. "Was it you?"

Freyja shook her head. "No, but rest assured I will find the assassin and send him to Hel where he belongs." In truth, Freyja already knew who fired the arrow, and she also knew the antidote to save Gunwald's life. But Freyja's soul was steeped in jealousy, and she could no longer stand to see the joy of love that bound Gunwald and Skuld, the same love shared by humans, an emotion unknown to her. "For Gunwald's life to be saved, you must give him three drops of your blood, Skuld, but that will not stop the poison of the silver running through his body."

A cut appeared on Skuld's wrist, and she held it over Gunwald's parted lips until three drops of blood fell into his mouth.

Gunwald's eyes fluttered open, and he stared with tenderness at his beloved. "Our souls will always be together, my love," he whispered.

Skuld leaned closer and kissed him.

"I also had a vision…," Gunwald continued. "The young woman you saw… I will be her scribe. Send me images of her life, and I will keep her stories safe. We must protect her." He sighed. "My dearest love… my Lady and the Rose."

Skuld looked to Freyja. "Give us something, or I swear I will call upon the Well of Urd and bring wrath to this place." She gasped between her sobs. "I beg of you, Freyja, please, allow us one cycle of the sun and stars. And in return I will bring back life to all that withers in the coldest times."

Freyja nodded. "Agreed. On the equinox, you and Gunwald shall be together as in your youth, without pain or age." Freyja gathered Gunwald in her arms.

"Maeve, Kelda, Selby," Skuld called to the fairies, and three ethereal beings appeared. "Go with my beloved and care for him. You shall have the freedom to go beyond the depths of his world, but please… look after my love." She glared at Freyja, who dared not question her demand.

The fairies nodded as they fluttered around Gunwald. "Yes, dearest Skuld," they answered in unison.

Hakon leaned over his father and kissed him lightly. "I will watch over Mother."

Gunwald laid a hand over Hakon's heart. "Always keep love in your heart."

Hakon nodded and stepped away.

Skuld's lips brushed Gunwald's, and as she lifted her head, he saw that her tears had turned to rose petals.

The corners of Gunwald's lips turned upward. "My sweet Lady and the Rose," he said, his words barely audible.

"My eternal beloved," Skuld said as she let go of Gunwald's hands.

Hakon caught his mother as she fell.

Freyja turned to Skuld just as a set of stone steps appeared in the snow, and for a moment an essence of something she had not known before washed over her.

Skuld raised her head and spoke without words to Freyja. *That is my heart breaking, Freyja. May you never feel this agony...*

Struck by the power of Skuld's raw emotion, Freyja turned away and quickly descended the stairs.

A blanket of snow washed away all visible traces of Skuld's beloved Gunwald and the secret world that lay below ice and snow. As she clung to her son, Skuld's desperate screams of pain echoed across the landscape.

ITH HER BELOVED gone, the Lady and the Rose, as Skuld came to be known, roamed the earth, tending to the brokenhearted, leaving behind a single rose, hoping that such beauty would give rise to a new day. Once a year the three fairies, Maeve, Kelda, and Selby, created a bedchamber filled with flowers and exotic sweet fruits, nectar, and a pool of warm, salted water scented with frankincense and rose petals, for Gunwald and the Lady to share during their time together. As Gunwald ascended the steps from where he lived, he gathered his beloved into his arms and together they disappeared into the boudoir where they remained for twenty-four hours.

Before Gunwald descended to his sanctuary, Hakon

would take time to speak with him, telling him news of the fae and the issues they faced.

"Thank you," Gunwald would say. "I am proud to call you my son."

"You are missed, Father," Hakon would reply and then turn away so his parents could say farewell in privacy.

After Gunwald and the fairies descended the staircase again, a gust of snow covered the entrance where it would lay undisturbed until the following year. And although Freyja was known for her strict decrees, she kept her promise and allowed the couple to communicate telepathically, for she also sensed her world changing and that thought brought with it a tinge of both excitement and fear.

Wherever she traveled, the Lady sent images to her beloved scribe. From Egypt, she brought him parchment, and Gunwald began recording events through drawings and the written word. He drew an image of a wooden horse—so large that men hid inside—and of a wolf who fed two human boys. Later he wrote about an empire of enormous power. He wrote of a massive wall—some 1,500 miles in length—built to protect one country from invasion by another; and of a leader—a woman named Cleopatra who loved two men; and a man who preached to others that he was the son of God.

The Lady observed wars as they came and went. The waning of belief in the gods and goddesses caused them to be forgotten and disappear into the clouds. Mortals came to believe in a single god, and that became a new religion. Fighting continued to be rampant, bound more now to religion than geography, or so the humans believed. Hakon took over from his father and worked to keep the fae safe and together in their northern lands. His task proved difficult as the threat of war in the name of a place called Heaven spread fear throughout the areas of the north. But Hakon persevered and protected his people, always placing them before his own needs, just as his father had done.

And then one day a few centuries before the year 1000, the Lady was drawn to a place far from her home where she observed a web of deceit and love unfold. She knew at that instant that her vision from long ago was about to unfurl. She closed her eyes and watched from afar as Hakon strode across the desolate tundra and suddenly froze. He looked around as if searching for something or someone. But the Lady and the Rose had also heard a young woman's cries for help as a familiar image flashed before her.

A woman, a sage from the northern lands, cried out from the remains of a storm-battered longship as gnarled fingers of black water stole her kinsmen and dragged them to the depths of the ocean.

A mist gathered around Hakon, and when it had dissipated the image of him was gone. The Lady spoke to Gunwald, telling him to be ready, for the story of their granddaughter was unfolding.

But all of that happened long ago. Gunwald kept his

word, and every day since the tainted arrow pierced his heart he has written the stories of the life of his granddaughter as seen through the eyes of his beloved Lady. The journals are kept safe in a place called Sanctuary.

CHAPTER 3

PRESENT DAY: SANCTUARY

T FIRST GLANCE, one would assume this room was a library, but those in the know called it Sanctuary. And if one tried to ascertain who looked after this place, well, it would be easy to brand the silver-haired gentleman strolling between the bookshelves as the holder of that title, but that would be a mistake. The role of bibliothecary in truth fell into the hands of fairies… fairies whose ancestors had emerged from the Forest of the Dryads way south of this land, but that was long ago, long before the last ice age.

While the titles inscribed upon the leather-bound books that crowded the many shelves in their thousands might appear familiar, the assemblage was anything but ordinary. For that specific collection of books was a constant work of alchemy, a never-ending story of sedimentary layers from mercurial events, twisting and turning and sometimes even brandishing moments of gold.

On one particular day, the scribe, as he referred to himself, gently stretched his tall frame in direct answer to the creaks echoing from above, the sounds a valid indicator that the vast room was in the process of expanding. Sanctuary was a living organism—it breathed and grew as a force of magic extended bookshelves and created new areas of study for the scribe, who had dedicated a large part of his life to one particular, ever-evolving story.

When the movement settled, the aged man walked over to a wooden table and eyed a plate of fruit and nuts. He lowered himself onto a chair and nibbled at the food. A faint buzzing sound—like the beating whirr of a hummingbird's wings—drew his gaze toward three ethereal apparitions cloaked in free-flowing garb.

The fairies dipped and dived in the air of the vast cavern before landing on the dark wood of the table to lift a delicate bone china teapot from which they poured an aromatic liquid. One of the fairies handed him a cup on a matching saucer, and he accepted her offer before inhaling the steam rising from the hot water.

"My favorite," he said. "Bergamot and lemon. Thank you, Maeve."

Another pulled a peacock feather tucked between the crease of her bosom and placed it on the table in front of him. She lowered her head, but it was too late, for the scribe saw the blush of her cheeks.

"Kelda," he said, picking up the feather, "have you been searching for Juno again?"

Kelda's cheeks were now a deep crimson as she bobbed her head up and down.

"And tell me," he continued, "did you find her?"

"No," Kelda said, her voice that of a woman's, not the young girl she appeared to be. "Do you like the feather, Gunwald?"

"Very much so. Thank you."

The fairies giggled and then flew off in different directions with feather dusters in hand, leaving Gunwald alone with his musings. They dusted shelves carved from the bedrock that lined the spacious grotto, then flittered around pillars—monoliths that stood twelve feet apart, etched with numbers denoting the passage of time—that reached up to the curved ceiling. The shelves were lined with leather-bound tomes, the volumes sacred, their pages revealing histories long forgotten. Many of the shelves were still empty, waiting to be filled with stories yet born.

It was left to Gunwald to catch wisps of one particular woman's life, which were collected by the sentinel known as the Lady and the Rose, who sent him thoughts and images telepathically. He then transcribed those moments into an extended memoir of sorts— the ongoing account of an immortal seer whose name changed countless times during her long life.

Often he could be found sitting at the edge of a warm crystalline pool surrounded by smooth rocks; he liked to write there, dangling his toes in the water and watching rainbows form over a small waterfall that seeped from somewhere above and cascaded onto the aqua body of water. Sometimes the words he wrote made him cry and the fairies would comfort him. This was one of those days.

"Why are you sad, Gunwald?" a fairy asked.

Gunwald wiped his eyes with the long sleeve of his robe. "Selby, it's…" He paused, collecting himself after a recent dispatch from the sentinel. "Our girl has lost another mortal friend to the next world," he said. "This friend was a good person, but she became lost. In a moment of weakness, evil, disguised as love, caught hold of her heart, and it was that illusion of love that caused her demise."

"Keep writing," the fairies said at the same time. "For after sadness, joy is often found."

He looked up at their gleaming faces. "Such is the tale of our dear Astridr's life."

The fairies nodded their heads and once again they spoke as one. "That is the way of stories."

Gunwald's mouth turned up in a soft smile. "Yes, dear friends, and it is also the fate of my work."

At other times, when the fairies had completed their bibliothecarial duties, they'd trim the scribe's silver hair. They allowed themselves a giggle from behind the bookcases as they peeked out at him bathing under the waterfall. They brought him fresh clothes scented with frankincense and sang songs to him from the world of their ancestors.

Gunwald had documented Astridr's story for centuries, and each evening after he transcribed her daily narrative, he wandered the aisles, remembering moments in time. His long, delicate fingers traveled over the spine of the earliest journal, a memory of the extraordinary woman's life catching him midstep.

"Ah," he said with a sparkle in his eyes. "I remember this day well."

The fairies hovered above him. "Yes. Please, please, please read this story to us."

"Again?"

The fairies sat together on top of the bookshelf, drawing in their diaphanous wings and grooming one another's hair. "Always."

"But this particular journal tells only of Astridr's family and the bloodline from whence her magic derived. Would you not rather hear of one of her adventures instead?"

"No," they said. "From the beginning, for we cannot fully enjoy her story without her history."

"You of all people should understand that, Gunwald," Kelda said, placing a hand on her hip.

Gunwald consented to their logic and opened the aged book. It contained a tale of lovers, pulled apart and threaded together, that created the extraordinary life of Astridr. When the spine opened, the fairies watched as his script, written in gold ink, floated from the pages and settled in the ether before his eyes. As he read, his appearance changed from that of an elderly gentleman to the handsome man of his youth, the man from the time when the story was born. His blue eyes glistened and the wrinkles of time dissolved from his face; he stood tall, and his voice caught the words before they disappeared, but not before they touched the heart of his beloved, the Lady who lived beyond Sanctuary.

On that eve, as Gunwald's voice seeped beyond Sanctuary and entwined solely with the Lady's spirit, her thoughts dissolved to another place, where the Legend of Astridr began.

"My sweet Gunwald," the Lady said, her voice a breathy whisper. "How I love to hear this story of Astridr's inception from your lips."

As the sun settled and the northern world became drenched in a polar twilight, the landscape was beautified with a phosphorescent glow that radiated a spectrum of multicolored tones across a vast sky. Crags reached for the stars like broken teeth, highlighted in a rainbow of color while a serene silence orchestrated the strange beauty of the place.

The Lady waved a hand over the ground, and the snow beside her took the shape of an armchair. She sat and listened to her beloved's voice drifting up from Sanctuary. She remembered another night eons ago when she watched her son disappear in a cloud of mist. That night a geomagnetic storm caused tones of blues and purples to paint the heavens, wrapping the soul of this elegant place into a prism of wondrous beauty.

In the distance, a solitary reindeer trotted across the

expanse of whiteness and called to his mate, picking up speed when she answered. As he bounded off, his hooves kicked up snow that fell into a nearby pool of water, forming ripples of spectacular colors. Enamored with the beauty surrounding her and the voice of her beloved caressing her soul, the Lady watched the rainbow of color dancing on the horizon. She breathed in Gunwald's scent of frankincense mixed with her soft perfume of roses as it drifted across the land to a faraway place that long ago was the heart of the world—a place of learning like no other, impenetrable to wars, but not resistant to magic and immortal beings.

CHAPTER 4
BYZANTIUM

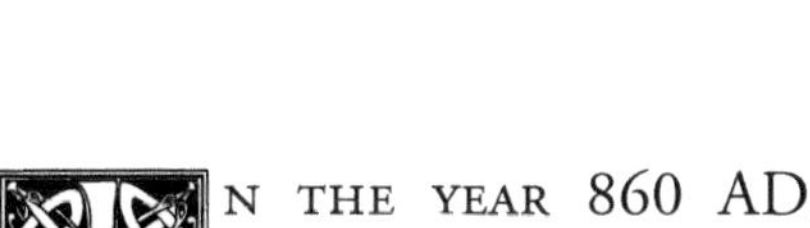

IN THE YEAR 860 AD, on the outskirts of Constantinople amid a beach of golden sands, a wave broke, and in its retreat it grasped a lacy collar of foam, dragging it back to the waters from whence it was born. Seagulls floating over a fisherman's haul mimicked the shrill notes of a piccolo, the melody of which was harmonized by human voices shouting orders around the hum of recently anchored boats.

Among the crowd of men was a trader with a ruddy face, folded eyelids, and copper-colored eyes. He puffed out his chest and clasped his hands behind his back as he observed his long-awaited goods before giving a dismissive nod to his workers as they unloaded his cargo. He turned to a man yelling orders, and with a click of his fingers, the trader caught the man's attention.

"Deliver this to my house." He pointed to a large

wooden crate filled with numerous ceramic amphorae. "The rest of the merchandise goes to the warehouse."

In the shadows of the waterfront buildings stood a pale-skinned immortal dressed in a tunic with long stockings bound to his legs, high leather boots, and a hooded cape. He'd watched the trader from a distance and wondered if the cargo the man awaited was far more valuable than the goods that had already arrived. The immortal had received word from the far north that a sage had been stolen, and though the reward of gold for helping her regain her freedom was not something he needed, it happened that he had a memory of the woman, for he knew her chief.

As a young girl, the sage had said to him, "Nikandros, you and my daughter will be great friends." It was that memory of Sonja that urged Nikandros to discover what he could about her whereabouts. His search had led him to a group of three men, one of whom was the trader. Nikandros sought out trusted allies within the city, and together they waited for the seer to arrive.

The trader raised his head and scanned the azure waters of the vast harbor, searching for a particular vessel, but in its absence, he drew back into the crowd. Leaving behind the stench of rotting fish and bawdry scoffs of men eager to explore the city, he strode through busy streets, surrounded by the clipped and animated voices of merchants peddling their wares and bringing life to the early morning. Grateful for the intoxicating smells of the market, he breathed in aromas of delicate spices and continued along a cobblestone alley before stopping in front of a lavish two-storied building, the door of which was adorned with a brass cross.

Unaware that the immortal Nikandros was watching him, the trader rested a hand on the door and considered the nonappearance of the soldiers who were under orders to kidnap the great seer from her northern homeland. He let out a heavy sigh before pushing open the door. When he entered the house, he found himself in a single room graced with a carpet of bright colors and ornately carved furniture.

His trading partner, the high-ranking Menas, was known for his fierce intolerance of anyone failing to carry out his orders. He rose from a chair, his bushy eyebrows lifted in expectation. Those brows folded in disappointment when the trader shook his head.

"Our ship does not grace the harbor today," the trader said.

Menas sank back into the chair. "I do not like this. Surely our men should have returned by now."

Another man, wearing robes of sumptuous silk, his sight obscured by cataracts, shook his head. "God will bring them home, for the treasure our soldiers search for holds more value than silk and gold."

"And is more difficult to attain," the trader said. "And if her chief suspects us, what then?"

A church bell tolled, and that brought a smile to Menas, who was wearing an ornately embroidered dalmatica and cloak. "We live in the Queen of Cities." He adjusted the heavily jeweled collar that rested on his shoulders, a reminder to all that he was a member of the elite. "Fear not, for no army of men can penetrate our vast walls."

The robed man turned to him. "It is not men who concern me, Menas, but those from a different world. I pray your wisdom has thought of the consequences of interfering in the world of spirit."

"We are men of influence," Menas replied. "Our city houses a splendorous domed temple, and signs of our faith adorn buildings. God will protect us." He placed a high value on Christian beliefs and reckoned that gold and faith would warrant his reward.

"I pray our ardent ambition has not led us down a path of darkness," the robed man said. He lowered his voice to a whisper. "And that the woman we seek has the prophecy to quell the rumors that a gathering army is preparing to advance on our city."

Having heard the entire conversation, Nikandros slipped into the lengthening shadows of day in search of his comrades.

CHAPTER 5

NORTHERN LANDS: SONJA'S STORY

FAR NORTH OF Byzantium, signs of spring had begun to push through snow-covered grounds, bringing a smile to a woman of great beauty as she began her daily pilgrimage from the village where she lived, through a forest, to a nearby cove. Sonja, known in those parts as the great seer, was born with the gift of preternatural sight; a childhood swathed with visions, many of which frightened her, for she saw death and destruction of loved ones and the land she called home. In her youth she witnessed her kin setting forth on long expeditions, knowing that some would return and others would not, and images of men fallen in battle, their bodies oozing blood. She saw men drowned in treacherous seas and others landing in faraway lands, never to return to their homeland.

Sonja had witnessed her mother's death twice; once as a vision, the other in real life. She had stayed with her father until he too passed to the next world, and then at eleven years of age, she entered the house of the chief of the village, and there she used her gift of sight to keep their community safe from plunder and disease for twenty-one years. Word of Sonja's prowess as a seer spread across the lands until, eventually, whispers of her rare gift and exceptional beauty reached the ears of men who sought extreme power. Sadly, her gift of sight made Sonja blind to the fate of certain aspects of her own life, but even the most foolish of seers understood the dangers of knowing all. And Sonja was not foolish.

Dawn was Sonja's favorite part of the day—the freshness of a new beginning, the crisp air, the untrodden paths. As she walked away from her village to the cove, Sonja found solace in listening to the crunch of ice and snow beneath her footsteps. She gazed up at the cloudy skies and rubbed her arms as a chill in the atmosphere prickled her skin. Breathing in the quiet solitude, she sought out the reason for her anxiety, anchoring her senses to the trees around her, searching for a clue, only to find emptiness.

When she reached the water's edge, she gazed across the bay toward the cliffs that marked the entrance to the ocean. Another breeze brushed past, this time catching her long golden hair as if wanting to guide her back to the safety of the village, for this time the wind carried a cautionary whisper and a sense of urgency.

Sonja turned to leave.

Five men stood before her, dressed in strange tunics adorned with metal, and capes trimmed with a fabric of vibrant colors and intricately patterned embroidery, the likes of which Sonja had not seen before. The uniformed men all bore swords—two were drawn, the point of one scarcely touching the bare skin of Sonja's neck, the other pointed at her solar plexus. She remained perfectly still.

One of the men spoke, but Sonja didn't understand his words.

"What do you want of me?" she asked, but the frown on the man's face told Sonja that, like her, he did not understand her words.

He nodded to another soldier, who stepped forward.

"You will come with us." He spoke her language, and although his words were broken and stilted, Sonja understood him.

"Where?"

"Constantinople," he said. "There are rumors of unrest outside our city's walls, and although we have spies among our enemies, we are unable to gather the information we need."

Caught in a clairvoyant moment, Sonja closed her eyes, and when they fluttered open, she stared at the first man who had spoken to her. "You take me from my home—from those I love—in the hope that I will prophesize the fate of your city," she said. "But I saw the man who sent you to find me. He does not care for you or any of his soldiers. He cares only for riches."

Her translator repeated her words, and anger passed over the leader's stern gaze. He rolled his shoulders and gave a quick, decisive nod to the two men closest to her. They grabbed her arms and tied her hands behind her back.

"You would do well to say farewell to your families," Sonja said. "And tell the man called Menas that I will never do as he asks!" Her words had brought fear to her captors, and that would not sit well with them.

They tied a length of fabric around her head, covering her mouth, and then hustled her through the forest, away from her village, until they reached the far end of the bay.

Secured to a tree and hidden by branches was a small boat. Sonja watched as two of the men pushed it into the water and settled at the oars. She shuddered as another lifted her into his arms and carried her to the boat, placing her inside before crouching beside her. Sonja's gaze darted across the fading landscape as the oarsman guided the craft away from the only home she had ever known.

When the vessel rounded the entrance to the cove, the men rowed hard against the current toward a large ship anchored off the coast. Sonja had never ventured on the open waters beyond her home, and although her heart pined for her kin, she marveled at the expanse of water surrounding the boat and how the sky and waters melted into each other in the distance.

From the sea, they traveled past land and along rivers

until, weeks later, exhausted from the journey, they arrived at a place unlike anything Sonja could have imagined. A community bustled with activity, the smells and colors unknown to her, and people with darker skin wore brightly colored apparel and conversed in a plethora of languages. As the soldiers led her along alleys paved with stone, Sonja noticed symbols displayed on buildings: a circle marked with crisscrossing lines, and crosses made of metal embellished with jewels. Sonja had heard of the symbol of the cross and of the man it represented. It was a strange concept to her, so distant from her pagan ideals.

Sonja shivered as a swish of color crossed her path, a woman in a cloak of blood-red fabric with threads of gold woven into the edges and hemline. Farther ahead a man swept cobblestones, the soles of his feet wrapped in leather and secured with straps around his ankles. The crowd cleared a path for the soldiers as they guided Sonja forward, past a building like nothing she had ever seen, its arches and domes reaching upward toward the sky. Sonja gazed up at the magnificent structure, and as she did, a vision flashed before her.

Fire on the outskirts of the city. Flames licking the sky. The acrid scent of burning flesh. Women and children fleeing their homes, racing toward the great domed place of worship. The clash of swords, howls of pain, and soldiers gasping their final breath before death. The mark of her kin chiseled into the stonework of a parapet.

A tug on her arm released her from the morbid scene and brought her back to her current existence.

The soldiers led her up an incline until she stood at the base of a high tower. She followed the men up winding stairs to a circular room with bedding, a chair, and a barred window; this was her prison.

When the door closed, Sonja moved to the window and gazed out at the expanse of buildings below. A series of never-ending alleys twisted and curved like a serpent throughout the city, lined with structures—some multistoried with tall rock walls encompassing gardens of exotic plants and trees—and sculptures carved from stone and surrounded by water. She watched the sun as it dipped over the domed building and melted into the waters beyond.

Sonja reached into the leather pouch that hung from a cord around her waist and enjoyed the familiarity of the touch of her sacred runes. "Do my people know where I am?" she whispered as she tossed the runes onto the dimpled stones of the windowsill. She closed her eyes, and a vision flooded her mind.

A soldier stands in the shadows of the inner walls of the city. He is approached by a tall man dressed in a black cape, the hood of which accentuates his pale skin, dark eyes and hair. The soldier wears a bronze ring—the intricate runic engravings tell of his northern lineage and are hidden from his so-called peers. He drops a key into the pale man's waiting palm. The two men clasp each other's elbows before going their separate ways and blending into the night.

Sonja, the great seer, opened her eyes, and a smile

brushed across her lips. She remembered the pale-skinned Nikandros from her childhood, for he was a friend of the chief of her village, and she pondered on the part he would play in her life. She twisted the bronze ring on her finger, thankful for the runic engravings that connected her to her kin. She held her head high, looked out across the harbor, and beheld the beauty of the sunset.

CHAPTER 6

GUARDIANS

ENAS STRODE ALONG the cobblestone alley to the tower that held the great seer hostage. Half a dozen soldiers stood guard, parting when their leader approached. One of them opened the door in anticipation of his superior, and once inside, Menas darted up the narrow spiral staircase to the landing where two more soldiers guarded the entrance. He gestured toward the door, and one of the guards unlocked the bolt. Menas entered, attended by the soldier who spoke Sonja's language. The door closed behind them.

The woman before him turned from where she gazed out the window, and a smirk crossed Menas's lips when he saw the seer's beauty. He studied her face, and then he looked over her body.

"I trust your journey was not too strenuous, my dear," he said. The soldier translated his words.

Sonja stared into his eyes but said nothing. Menas stepped closer, placed a hand under her chin, and took in the seer's beauty. "The stories of your beauty do not do you justice, and I wonder… what do you see in my future?" When Sonja remained silent after the translation, Menas ran a finger from her chin, down her neck, to the edge of the fabric that covered her body. "Perhaps you will do better with another question. Is there truth to the rumors of an army gathering to attack this city?"

Sonja stared at him, her emerald-green eyes searing like a hot spear into his soul. When she spoke, her words were in the language of her people—poetry not yet written—and although Menas did not understand her, there was no mistaking the prickling of his skin and the sense of impending doom that ran up his spine.

"Be only a little wise," she whispered, "never too wise, and best not to ask your fate but to live a happier life without knowing."

There was no need for translation, for by the power of intuition and a touch of magic, Menas understood the sage perfectly. When he saw his hand trembling, he lowered his arm and walked to the door.

"Open!" he demanded.

He fled the tower as beads of sweat gathered above his upper lip and the hair lifted on his nape and arms. He had an urge to feel in control of something, someone, and as the fading light brought shadows across his path, he thought of the woman who awaited him. Yes, the prostitute would pay for the seer's undisciplined display of authority.

Nikandros had watched Menas enter and leave the tower, his preternatural senses having allowed him to hear the conversation between Sonja and her captor. Turning toward the ocean, he relished the cool evening breeze as it blew across the great city, catching the scent of spiced meats cooking on hearths and the rich coppery scent of human blood.

A woman clad in a cloak of blood-red fabric trimmed with threads of gold climbed swiftly across the roofline and crouched beside Nikandros.

"Did you see the northern warriors?" he asked.

The woman nodded. "Yes. It is as if the gods have answered their call, for their longships are hidden under a cloud of fog."

"When darkness covers the city, go to the top of the wall and swing a lantern three times," he said. "Then—"

"I will take care of Menas's men. You need not be concerned."

Nikandros turned to her. "Remember, Menas and the trader are mine."

CHAPTER 7

RESCUE AND DEATH

N ARMY OF Vikings anchored in a deserted harbor of the Sea of Marmara and watched as their kinsmen, a crew of thirteen elite warriors, beached their ship and waited for the signal from an insider that a gate at the edge of the impenetrable Theodosian Walls was open. The thirteen men slipped into the vast city of Constantinople under a curtain of darkness and magic. With their landing blessed by the sliver of a crescent moon hidden by foreboding clouds, they seemed invisible to their enemy, their task consecrated by the gods. As the warriors worked their way stealthily over stone walls and along cobblestone alleys, their mission stayed focused on a tower they knew to be heavily guarded.

Caught off guard, the Byzantine soldiers had little time to deflect the assault of the bare-chested and brawny Nordic men. Wielding swords marked with the *Ulfberht* name, each pommel engraved with the symbol of three crescent moons, the men showed no mercy, never stopping until the bloodstained bodies of the Romans littered the periphery of the tower. The melee was over in minutes. Wasting no time, the men battered down the thick wooden door that barred the entrance to the tower and then charged up the winding steps to a landing, bringing swift deaths to the two soldiers stationed there.

The leader of the warriors, a burly man whose muscular body glistened with sweat and splatters of blood, pulled an ax from his belt, and with two mighty blows the lock broke away. He pushed the door open.

Opposite stood a tall woman with long golden hair and stunning emerald-green eyes. She wore a pale pink linen underdress and a crimson woolen smock kept in place with gilt bronze shell-shaped brooches. Around her waist lay a belt made of woven leather, decorated with sea-glass beads, upon which hung a leather pouch.

The warriors bowed their heads in respect, and the leader took a step toward her. "We are here to take you home," he said, speaking the language of his Nordic homeland.

"Yes," she answered, her voice sweet-sounding, tender, and composed amid the tension of escape. "I have seen the one who guided you here."

Sonja gathered the stones marked with ancient symbols from the windowsill and placed them in the leather pouch. With a last glance around the room, she laid an earth-toned woolen cloak over her shoulders and then followed the warriors down the spiral stairs, through deserted alleys, to the beach where their ship lay waiting.

But from the moment they had left the tower, a sense of anxiety crept up Sonja's spine, and yet no visions of death fell before her. As she stepped onto the waiting boat, she turned to the leader. "Do you have reason to be concerned with our journey?"

The warrior shook his head. "No." He looked up at the clearing skies. "We are men of the sea; she is in our blood and we do not fear her."

Placing a hand on his arm, Sonja hoped for insight; however, when none came she boarded and watched as the warriors rowed the boat out past the other long-ships and led the way northward.

But Sonja's fears were not amiss, for what the gods had in mind for her was more momentous than the life of a seer. The sky dimmed to dark indigo, and thunderclouds spread like ink across the horizon. The sea roared, and coal-colored waves crashed against the boat, their white tips seizing the men and dragging them, one by one, into the depths of the icy waters.

Sonja screamed at her gods. "Take me, not these brave souls, for they have risked their lives to rescue me." Her golden hair, once bright like the sun's rays, now hung around her face in salt-lathered, twisted curls. Her deep-set forest-green eyes had lost their luster and were now teary and veiled behind her sad resignation.

However, to secure her safety the Viking men had tied their sage to the most substantial part of the boat. When the last of her kin had drowned, the winds subsided and the sky and sea became a slate of gray, and Sonja succumbed to the pull of exhaustion and fell asleep, alone, hungry, and parched from thirst.

CHAPTER 8

RETRIBUTION

NIKANDROS OBSERVED THE crate filled with ceramic amphorae and then leaped up to the balcony where the scent of the trader was most potent. He entered a bedroom and strode toward where the man rested. The trader reached for a dagger on the floor, only to find it gone. In one quick motion, Nikandros dragged the man from his bed. The trader kicked at him, but his efforts were in vain.

"You've stolen for the last time," Nikandros said.

In a frantic attempt to free himself from Nikandros's powerful grip, the trader directed a punch at his head, but Nikandros dodged the blow and the trader slumped in defeat. The visible pulse throbbing in the trader's neck captured the immortal's attention.

"Enjoy your final voyage," he said and squeezed the trader's neck until the popping of bones and stench of bodily fluids told him death had come to his victim.

Outside, the soldier waited for him, and Nikandros tossed a key into his friend's waiting palm. "Distribute the goods to those in need."

The soldier wrapped his fingers around the key. "Consider it done."

The men clasped elbows.

"Thank you, my friend," Nikandros said before disappearing along the alley and into the darkness.

Later, when Nikandros entered a two-storied house, his senses alerted him to the musky scent of sex lingering in the air. Grunts of pleasure floated to the lower floor, and he made his way up the stairs to a room where his prey lay on a bed, wearing only his jeweled collar while a woman pleasured him with her mouth.

Sensing the intrusion, the woman sat up and grinned at the naked man before her. "It is time for me to leave, Menas."

Menas grabbed her wrists. "You will leave when I say."

"No," Nikandros said, "she will leave now." In a flash, he had Menas pinned against a wall. He yanked the heavily jeweled collar from Menas's neck and tossed it at the woman. "Thank you."

The woman caught the collar. "Think nothing of it, Nikandros," she said and left the room, carrying her clothes and the jewelry.

Nikandros turned his attention to the trembling man in his clutches. "Did you think you were above deception, Menas?" he said, his voice callous and dripping with hatred.

Spittle dripped from his victim's mouth, and his eyes bulged as his body fought for breath.

Nikandros ran his tongue over his lips, and the tips of sharp fangs glistened in the moonlight that crept through a window. "You stole a woman—and that is a crime. Your punishment is death."

He plunged his fangs into the bulging vein on Menas's neck and drank until he sensed the final beat of the cruel man's heart. He tossed the lifeless body to the floor and strode outside.

Waiting for him in the shadows was a tall woman, the leather tunic of a warrior barely visible beneath her red cloak. "Is it done?" she asked Nikandros as he approached.

He answered with a quick nod. "Has the third conspirator been disposed of?"

"Yes."

Placing his hands either side of her shoulders, Nikandros searched the woman's sad eyes. "Not all men are cruel, Sabine," he said. "You have my word that while I live in this immortal body, I shall protect you, do you understand?" Sabine nodded and Nikandros took her hand. "Come. It is time for us to leave this city. I am feeling the pull of my home in Salerno."

They walked along the dark streets, climbed easily over the mighty Theodosian Walls, and left the city of Constantinople behind them.

CHAPTER 9

HAKON

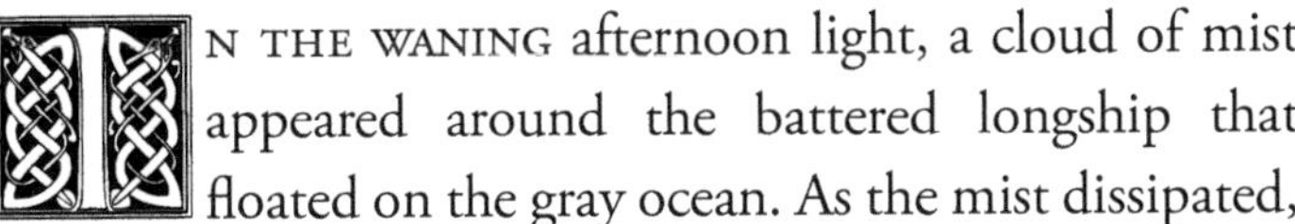

I N THE WANING afternoon light, a cloud of mist appeared around the battered longship that floated on the gray ocean. As the mist dissipated, a man stepped forward and gazed in adoration at Sonja. The man's stature was tall and robust, and his snow-white hair was pulled back and tied loosely with a strip of leather. But it was his eyes that showed he was not of the mortal world, for they bore the golden hue of the sempiternal fae prince, Hakon.

He wore the clothes of an elfin warrior. A leather tunic embedded with chain mail lay under a floor-length leather coat adorned with wide wrist cuffs and pauldrons of intricately engraved metal plates. Dark leather straps wrapped around his long boots and continued up over his leather pants. A thick belt hung low on his hips, and a baldric held the scabbard that bore his sword, its hilt emblazoned with the warrior rune *teiwaz*. Over his shoulder hung a yew bow. Arrows with shafts marked with runes flickered in the light and waited in readiness in a well-worn quiver.

He cupped the seer's chin with his hand and dampened her parched lips with fresh water from a goblet that materialized in his hand. "Sweet lady of the mystic world," he said, his voice a hushed velvet whisper. "Drink this water borne of the snowmelt and the clouds that hang above the blanket of high glaciers. Remember the softness of the moss beneath your feet, taste the morning dew upon your face, and envision the magic of my kind within the arch of colors spread over the earth where you once walked. These are the gifts our land brings forth. Do not step into the next realm; take my hand and I will guide you on your journey home."

Gunwald peered up at the fairies, whose eyes remained glazed with concentration. "May I have some tea?"

Maeve swiftly flew toward the far end of Sanctuary and returned bearing a tray with a teapot, cup, and saucer. She placed the service on a nearby shelf, poured the steaming liquid into the cup, and fluttered over to Gunwald.

He breathed in the steam and grinned at Maeve. "My favorite," he said, with a wink. "Burdock and mint."

Maeve arched a brow and tilted her head to one side. "Are you hungry?" she asked, handing him the refreshment.

Gunwald shook his head. "No, thank you. The tea is all I need for now."

Maeve returned to settle beside Kelda and Selby while Gunwald sipped on the hot beverage. A heavy sigh from above brought the scribe's attention to the fairies, and he noticed Kelda had stretched out along the top of the bookshelf, her head resting on the palm of her hand.

"Are you bored, Kelda?" he asked.

"No," she said. "I am impatient."

"Have you finished with your tea?" Maeve asked.

"Almost," Gunwald said and shortly placed the teacup and saucer on a nearby shelf. "Now, where were we?"

"Hakon is about to kiss her," the fairies said in unison.

The corners of Gunwald's mouth turned upward. "Not quite." He waved a hand and the gold script floated from the page, and he began to read once more. "On an island close to Sanctuary and yet far away and in a world of its own is a place marked by death and darkness."

"This is the scary part," Kelda said, snuggling close to Selby.

"Freyja has a part to play in our world, Kelda," Gunwald said. "And although her realm can seem dark and daunting, like all realms, hers is needed."

"Have you been there?" Selby asked.

Gunwald nodded. "Yes, long ago… Now, may I continue, ladies?"

The fairies nodded in agreement.

CHAPTER 10

FREYJA

IGH ABOVE THE cliffs that marked the entrance to the River Styx lay the fortified castle of Freyja, the goddess of the underworld. Towers of granite loomed hundreds of feet above obsidian cliffs and reached toward dark, swirling clouds that steadily hovered above the island. Violent waves crashed against worn rocks and performed a cacophony of deafening blasts, sending plumes of salty spray into the frigid atmosphere.

From a stone balcony adjoining the tallest turret of her bastion stood Freyja, a picture of magnificence in all her strength and elegant darkness. Her long raven-hued hair was caught in a sudden gust of wind and pulled this way and that until the strands unfolded around her head like a feathered fan.

A symphony of thunderous booms echoed through the jagged fjord, marking the entrance to Freyja's domain.

The familiar sound of waves crashing against rocks hundreds of feet below reminded their mistress that the boatman, Charon, was on his way to gather another soul.

Freyja held up a hand. "Be still!" In that instance, silence fell upon her domain. A vision played out before her.

The great seer and the fae prince stand together on a battered boat in the middle of an ocean.

Freyja lowered her hand, orchestrating the waves to rise and fall at her command while the wind picked up in intensity.

A nudge at her ankles reminded her of what she must do. "Yes, my darling," she said, her voice steely and controlled. "It seems the gods have answered my wishes. Let us see if the young prince's love is made of the same strength as his parents'."

Freyja lifted a black cat above her head and stared into the feline's beady black eyes. "Fly!" she whispered. She tossed the cat high into the air and watched it morph into a falcon. The bird of prey circled her, and as it dipped closer, Freyja leaped into the air, becoming one with the bird.

The falcon shrieked as she flew once around the foreboding fortress before pulling in her wings and soaring with the currents of the air, screeching as she dived toward the ocean and then leveled out twenty feet above the whitecaps. The falcon glided past islands and the mainland, across the open waters, until she spread her wings and circled above the speck of a ruined vessel.

As the bird descended, its form morphed back into that of the goddess, and she landed silently on the battered planks of the longship. Nestled in her hands was the beady-eyed black cat. Freyja, goddess of the underworld, had arrived to claim the Nordic seer.

CHAPTER 11

THE ACCORD

AKON HAD SENSED Freyja's presence long before she approached. Now, as she stood before him, he rose to his full height and stood protectively beside Sonja, for Freyja's composed expression did little to hide her intent.

"While her heart is still beating I lay claim to this woman," he said.

Freyja's expression echoed her resolute position as she waved toward an approaching veil of mist. "But Charon's boat cannot return to my realm empty," she said. "You know that, Hakon." She took a step closer to her victim.

Hakon placed an arm across Sonja's body. "There are dead men plenty on the ocean floor. Surely one of their souls will suffice."

Freyja's chuckle caused an ominous wave to grow in

strength around them. "I need an equal sacrifice—an ordinary man for a seer is hardly fair."

"The warriors who died today protecting their sage are anything but ordinary."

The goddess glared at the fae prince. "Your dedication to mortals is not something I understand, nor ever will. I stand firm in my decision. The seer is mine."

"Then what do you feel would be a fair exchange?" he asked. "For I will not leave Sonja with you, so what is it that you desire from me? We have known each other too long to waste time playing games when human lives are at stake."

Freyja gazed across the foreboding water at the advancing mist and then turned to Hakon. "I want to experience the truest human emotion," she said, taunting him as she urged a large wave to gather over the battered ship. "I want to experience love."

Hakon frowned and shook his head. "You know that cannot be, Freyja. As a goddess, your emotions remain restricted to your position. Love would cloud your ability to harness the dead, especially the damned. Love is a human attribute—"

"And yet you feel it!" Freyja cut in. "And the Lady and Gunwald!"

"Yes," Hakon said. "The fae have this gift, and we value it above all else. Courage and love made thirteen Viking warriors risk their own lives to save the woman standing beside me, and for that love, they have died. Their wives and children understood the sacrifice they made when their men departed from our shores, and now they will endure pain. The pain of loss, of death, is infinite. You cannot begin to fathom the agony of such suffering, Freyja, nor could you survive it."

Freyja considered Hakon's words and dropped her hand, making the wave crash directly behind Hakon. "You are correct," she said with a sneer. "I cannot comprehend such emotion. Tell me, how does love feel?"

Hakon gazed at Sonja with adoring eyes and then looked upward to the dusk sky. "Soon millions upon millions of stars will appear in the darkness," he said. "Alone, they are but one star—together, they form images bright enough to guide sailors and shepherds home to safety, to give explorers the knowledge to discover new lands. This eve the stars of Gemini guided me away from my lands. They guided me here, beside this lady, and she has stolen my heart. For the first time in my long life, I have found solace, and my heart is overflowing with love for this woman. I will keep her safe always. That is how love feels. Please do not steal this from me. One such loss in my family is enough."

Freyja raised an eyebrow at Hakon's last words.

They stood in silence until the veil of night surrounded them.

"If I were human, would there be a star to guide me to my beloved?"

"I do not doubt it," Hakon answered.

Freyja stepped close to him, her eyes narrowed, and she lowered her voice. "I do not trade souls."

"You saved my father," Hakon said. "Or was that something you planned all along?"

Another wave crashed beside the boat. "You may be a prince, but you are an insolent boy!"

"Perhaps I am, but I know better than to trust you."

"There is something I desire." She raked her gaze over Hakon's body and then chuckled. "When the time is right, make me human."

Hakon stared at her. "What you ask would break our rules."

Freyja stepped closer, within reaching distance to Sonja. "Then break them for once, or I shall take this woman's soul."

"And what happens to this world when your heart breaks?" he asked. "For you cannot stay in the human world."

"Then like all reasonable agreements, we shall have an amendment," she said. "If you see my essence dying, I give you permission to take the memory of love away from me, and I will return to my world."

Hakon's golden eyes clouded over, his mind seeming to be caught up in a turbid thought. Finally he nodded and sighed. "You see, this is what love does. I cannot let Sonja die, and yet I see a shadow of unfathomable sadness lingering over you in far-off times. You and I may not always agree, but we are, if nothing else, kindred spirits of immortality."

"Yes, Hakon, we are," Freyja said, taking a step back. "When will this happen?"

"I have waited eons for Sonja," Hakon said. "Love does not have a schedule." He placed his hands on her shoulders and kissed her forehead, sealing their agreement. "When the time comes, you will have the gift of humanity for a short while, and you will know love and be loved." He stared into her eyes with compassion. "But remember, as you are a goddess, I cannot allow your essence to wilt from a broken heart, and if I sense that happening, I shall remove all memories of love and your beloved."

And so it was that the fae prince and the goddess came to an agreement.

The wind picked up and a thick mist descended. The splash of oars hitting the water announced that the boatman was near.

"Rise, my brave children," Freyja announced.

In answer to her call, the thirteen elite warriors who gave their lives to rescue Sonja rose from the depths of the ocean.

From out of the mist a figure emerged, standing tall at the helm of an old and stable boat, his body draped in a piece of roughly woven crimson fabric, his silver hair billowing around his face.

The warriors walked upon the surface of the ocean, and one by one they climbed aboard the boat. Charon turned toward Freyja, his pale eyes devoid of emotion, the only color borne by his irises a ghostly white.

Freyja tossed a coin that landed in the boatman's waiting palm. She looked over her shoulder at Hakon.

"They are warriors, and therefore they are my children," she said. "You need not worry about these brave souls, for I will give them seats of honor."

Hakon watched as Freyja floated over to the boat and took her place at the helm. With oars in place, Charon turned the vessel around and headed back toward Freyja's realm.

CHAPTER 12

THE LOVERS

ONJA AWAKENED TO the warm touch and elemental omnipresence of the fae prince. Days and nights passed, and all the while Hakon sat on the raft he had constructed, Sonja's head resting in his lap. He gave her nourishment and sang the songs of their homeland.

> *Yonder lies a place of beauty,*
> *Blest by the moon,*
> *Born from limbs of Yggdrasil,*
> *Life immortal.*

> *'Twas on the eve of Winter Nights,*
> *When first their love was born,*
> *Two souls who are no more asunder,*
> *Glorious their love.*

Before the gods they swore their love,
Two hearts are now as one,
The heav'ns filled with light alluring,
Bound eternally.

Yonder lies a place of beauty,
Blest by the moon,
From their love a bairn was born,
Love for evermore.

Winters pass'd, their son grew strong,
But too the world did change,
Blood was spill'd upon the earth,
Lovers torn apart.

The king of fae, a scribe at heart,
The Lady, a guardian be,
Their son, a prince and warrior,
Bound forevermore.

Sonja reached toward Hakon and placed her hands either side of his face. "My prince," she whispered. "You have found me."

Their kiss carried them to a place of eternal love. And then, in the middle of the ocean, with the moon as their witness, Hakon gathered Sonja into his arms and gave her his love.

That evening the stars glowed brightly, and Hakon sensed the tug of time and the call of the northern lands.

"What is it, my love?" Sonja asked.

He kissed her temple and pulled her closer. "I must return to my homeland, for there is unrest among the fae," he said. "But first I shall find a safe place for you and return during the ebb of impending wars."

Sonja gazed up at the stars and shared with him a vision. "I have seen glimpses of the future where the people of the north no longer remember the joy of song and dance, or our poetry; it will be ripped away from our culture, replaced with a religion based on fear and guilt."

Hakon nodded. "I too have seen this. Denied their freedom to create as they wish, our kin will lose their joy for life and death and forget about their rituals. Ancient trees and sacred places will be desecrated, and with that tragic loss will appear the end of my realm as we know it." He leaned upon an elbow and gazed into Sonja's eyes. "You and I have created a being to walk among humanity, and she will protect those who keep balance in the world and see the magic in creativity. Our child will need the traits of the fae and the sight of a great sage, and because of you, my love, our daughter's beauty and powers will be unmeasured."

Their lips met, and the two lovers lost themselves in the essence of love and passion, under the stars of Gemini in the middle of a quiet ocean until the soft light of dawn reflected on the water.

ISLAND OF THE CRESCENT MOON

WHEN THE MYSTICAL Island of the Crescent Moon came into view, Hakon brought forth the winds to push the raft into a sheltered cove where he knew his beloved Sonja would be safe. As it happened, a colony of women had founded the island as a refuge from the wars of men, a hidden place where they were free to honor their pagan ways. Two of these women, who were on their way to a festival celebrating the cycle of the moon, discovered Sonja among splintered boards on the black sand. When they saw the strange woman with her white skin and sun-bleached hair, they believed her to be of great importance and welcomed her into their circle.

There would be times in the future when loneliness

clawed at her heart, making Sonja question if her time with Hakon had been a dream, only to be reminded of its authenticity by the growing life in her womb, for it soon became clear that Sonja was with child although no man had set foot on the island within living memory. While her belly grew with the phases of the moon, the women gave thanks to Juno, the goddess of fertility and childbirth. When Sonja fell into the throbbing pains of labor, the most experienced midwives of the village guided the child into the world of air and light.

The baby inhaled and opened her eyes, which were the color of the Etruscan sun and flecked with gold. She did not cry. The midwives gathered around her, gripped by awe, and later the elders bestowed high honors on the babe, for the hue of her eyes was considered divine among their people.

To further mark the importance of the child's birth, a black jaguar was born at the same time on the grounds of the Temple of Juno. Much to the surprise of the midwives, Sonja knew about the animal's birth and requested that it be brought to her to suckle from her breasts.

When asked why she would allow an animal to do such a thing, she explained her prophecy. "With the gift of my milk, the newborn animal will be freed from her strict corporal form by the power of the sages. This feline will become a magical creature—a shape-shifter, and she will protect my child."

On the eve of the infant's birth, while the women of the village lay sleeping, Hakon went to his beloved Sonja. He watched while she slept and then turned his attention to the tiny babe. Placing an amethyst stone into the palm of his daughter's hand, he whispered the legacy of his world.

"Look for the color of this stone—it will be seen in the eyes of those who must remain safeguarded above all else," he said. "They are the Creatives. But there will be one Creative who will have the gift of prophecy and also a touch of magic pulsing through her blood—you shall recognize her, but she will resist her gifts. Place this stone against her heart, and it will begin her transformation. Remember, little one, without balance our world is in danger of falling into chaos and everlasting darkness."

He closed the baby's fingers around the stone and kissed them. When she opened her tiny hand, the stone had vanished. Hakon turned his attention to Sonja, brushing loose strands of her lustrous hair away from her face.

Sonja stirred in her sleep. "Hakon, my love," she whispered. "Is this another dream?"

He took her hands and pressed them against his heart. "No, my beloved, I am here. And know that in spirit, I am always with you, for it is you who gives my heart its pulse."

"Will you stay with us now?"

Hakon kissed her fingers. "I will be with you until the birds sing their morning songs," he said, "and return once more when our daughter is old enough to understand her powers. On that day we will travel together to our homeland."

"I have seen you in my dreams," she said. "I know your heart aches for us, but do not be sad, my love, for last night the stars shared with me a vision of our future. Away from the sands and heat, back to our lands in the north where the waters run cold and clear beneath the icy blue of glaciers, of a place where the stories of our daughter are kept safe from the outside world." She raised her head and kissed him.

Hakon lay beside mother and babe until sleep lulled them into the dream world. He blanketed them in layers of protective spells, and when the birds began their morning song, Hakon kissed his beloved and departed to confer with the goddess Juno.

From behind his back, Gunwald revealed the peacock feather Kelda had given him, and reaching upward, he handed it to her. "If I remember correctly," he said with a twinkle in his eyes, "the following narrative is your favorite part of this journal. Am I correct, Kelda?"

A wash of color blossomed over Kelda's cheeks. She nodded her head and smiled. "Yes. Please, continue, Gunwald."

"Of course," he replied, and once again the gold script drifted from the page to rest before him.

CHAPTER 14

THE ALLEGIANCE

UNO AND HAKON, goddess and fae prince, met atop a cliff on the island at the temple of her sanctuary. Deep below the granite were frescoed caves that sheltered the entrance to a hidden tunnel. This path existed for the women of the Island of the Crescent Moon, a place to protect them should their lives ever be in peril.

Juno moved with a grace similar to the peacocks that walked beside her. Her dark eyes, lined with gold and white, mirrored the stare of the regal birds. Upon her head lay a diadem adorned with fresh white lilies and roses, and a robe of sheer white flax fell in folds over her body. When the goddess spoke, her voice echoed the sweet-sounding tones of a dawn breeze in summer. "You chose her mother well," she said. "For your daughter's gifts are great. Her journey will be a difficult one—immortal lives always are—and her destiny includes heartache, loss, and deep sorrow." Juno had also seen a vision in which the ways of her people were dishonored, and she understood the importance of the fae prince's babe.

"You know too well that it was the stars who guided me to Sonja. When I heard her cry for help across the ocean, I could not turn away," Hakon said. "As for our daughter's journey being troubled—all lives, immortal and mortal, are difficult—you and I know that only too well." He let his words hang in the ether for a moment, as if knowing they would be echoed by another man, another leader, in a different time, and the thought reminded him of the importance of relationships. "My daughter will need great love and a child of her own," he continued. "Can you give her these gifts?"

Juno looked up into the dark sky and drew in a deep breath. "Yes. She will have both lover and child, and another immortal already watches over her," she said. "Your daughter is under our providence, but I will not take away her human will and free spirit, for she will need those traits in her darkest times."

"Yes," Hakon said. "I, too, have seen the shadow of darkness, how it creeps into mortals' lives, luring them into a false sense of happiness. And when those too weak with despair collapse into the arms of evil, the light of joy is gone."

"You are like your father," she said. "Perhaps you are also a scribe."

A peacock spread out its feathers, displaying an arc of elegance. The corners of Juno's mouth tipped upward in a smile. "Joy cannot die as long as there is beauty in this world, Hakon," she said. "And you and I have seen the exceptional artistry humanity is capable of creating. Those who create art must have protection. You have seen this too, my friend."

Hakon nodded. "Yes, all Creatives—artists with the gift of prophecy—must be protected from evil."

A piece of parchment appeared in Juno's hands; she picked up a feather from the ground and dipped the quill in droplets of blood that seeped from a slight cut in her wrist. She began to write.

Creatives—artists with the gift of prophecy—

are now protected from the talons of darkness

by a cluster of immortal and mortal women and men.

These warriors shall be known as the Allegiance,

And will be led by the ethereal keeper.

Her name is Astridr—daughter of the fae prince Hakon,

and Sonja, the great Nordic seer.

All who enter the Allegiance will honor these words.

sine virtute omnia sunt perdita

(without courage, all is lost)

Juno signed her name and watched as Hakon drew blood to his wrist, soaked the quill, and signed his name beside hers.

CHAPTER 15

ASTRIDR

A S THE MOON lapsed into a pace of amaranthine phases, the Island of the Crescent Moon nurtured the women who resided upon her shores. Astridr grew to understand the gifts entrusted to her, and Sonja taught her the way of the seer, watching with pride as her daughter embraced the knowledge bestowed upon her.

On the birth celebration of Astridr's sixteenth year, Sonja observed her daughter from a distance as Astridr stood by the Temple of Juno and stared out across the vast ocean. When she fell into the thrall of a vision, the young woman's magic pulsed outward from her core in a surge of golden shards of light. Her power had manifested into something exorbitantly stronger than Sonja's, a supreme gift from the fae prince's blood that ran through their daughter's veins, and her grand-mother's, the Lady and the Rose.

Astridr wore a finely woven white linen chiton that denoted her as a daughter of a high priestess, and the flowers in her hair showed she was of age to leave the island. Her long white hair danced around her angelic face in rhythm with the wind, and as the sun melted into the horizon, rays of light were mirrored in her golden eyes.

During her visions, Astridr had seen men in bulky armor land on the beaches of the crescent-shaped island. Blood would stain the earth, but she would return in time to warn the women, giving them ample opportunity to flee to the land across the sea. The warriors would steal ancient artifacts and leave the women without the protection of their gods and goddesses, and in the new realm, they would feel fear, loneliness, and a life void of purpose.

When at last the moon rose into the darkening sky and visions of death and torture had ceased to torment her, Astridr turned and walked to her mother.

"Father is near," she said. "Go with him, Mother, back to the land of your birth. My heart is sad, and I am already lonely, but I have accepted my fate."

Sonja embraced her daughter. "There is an immortal named Nikandros… he helped me once, although in essence I believe he may have been protecting you. He is a friend to be trusted." She removed the ring from her finger and placed it on the middle finger of her daughter's right hand. "He will know you by this ring. As for us, well, we shall see each other again, sweet child. My

love is in your soul for eternity—remember my words during the times when your heart aches." Sonja draped a cape that she had woven over her daughter's shoulders and secured it with a tie. "The precious writings of the Allegiance are sewn into this fabric. This cape will protect you, just as you will protect those who create beauty and truth in this world." She cupped Astridr's face in her hands and brushed the tears that brimmed in her daughter's eyes. "When the time arrives for us to be together again, I will come to you in a dream and hand you the rune *raido*." She kissed her daughter and stepped back.

In that moment the world became silent and still. A mist rose around them, and Hakon stepped forward. He pulled Sonja to his chest. "It is time, my love," he said. "I need you by my side, for the ways of our people have been ravaged by fear and blood. We must gather our strength and return when the balance between good and evil is once again in danger of being forgotten." He turned to Astridr. "You are the essence of your mother's inner and outer beauty, and through her you are a powerful seer. From me, you have the gifts of the fae and the sight of destiny. Use them wisely. Your journey will not be an easy one—that is the way of gods and heroes. Always know you are loved, Astridr." He embraced her and kissed her forehead. "You are our greatest joy."

The young woman looked up at her father. "Will I find others like me?"

"There is no other being like you," he said.

"However, you have my word that you will not take this journey alone. Friends will guide you, and in time you will also find true love, of that I assure you."

Astridr placed her parents' hands in hers, and together they quoted the motto of the Allegiance. "*Sine virtute omnia sunt perdita.*" She lowered her hands, turned, and made her way back to the temple. A large black jaguar followed in her footsteps, and Astridr stopped and placed a kiss on its head. "I have an endless journey before me, my dearest friend. If you wish to stay here at the temple, I will understand. Juno will care for you." In a show of love, the animal butted her head against Astridr's body and then loped beside her as they continued their journey.

When they reached the temple grounds, Astridr knelt beside the jaguar. "I have wished that you would come with me, my dear, sweet Algiz," she said. "With you by my side, I have unending courage and faith, for you and I will always share unconditional love."

Standing at the edge of the cliff, Astridr tilted her face to the sky and raised her hands above her head. She focused on the immortal her mother had told her of—a powerful man who drank the blood of his enemies, a man who would guide her in the ways of the world beyond the island. A mist crept up from the ocean and slid silently over the temple until the tips of Astridr's white hair was all to be seen. A flash of light jolted through the sky, and Astridr and Algiz disappeared.

Hakon guided Sonja along the steep path that led to the small bay. The raft that had carried them to the island sixteen years ago now stood strong and sturdy and ready to return them to the icy waters of their homeland. They stepped onto the brittle boards, and Hakon called to the wind. Gentle gusts carried the two lovers into the mist left by their daughter's magic. The fae prince held his beloved in his arms and kissed her deeply. When he released her, the ice-covered, ragged mountains of their homeland peaked above the fog that bound the battered coastline.

"Home," whispered Sonja. With love in her heart, she gazed into her beloved's golden eyes. "Will she find us?"

Hakon smiled at his love and nodded his head. "When the ice from our mountains turns to water and the depths of the earth are in danger of being plundered, yes, Astridr will find us."

CHAPTER 16

FRIENDS

O N A MOUNTAIN high above the city of Salerno, Nikandros stared across the ocean as a bolt of lightning lit up the sky on the horizon. He did not know why he had chosen to return to this city by the sea, only that he had been guided by a series of mercurial events. Recently he had dreamed of a woman with skin like translucent alabaster and strange eyes—white irises framed with a background of ice-flowing water. In his dreams she had led him to the mountain where he now stood. In answer to his thoughts, he caught the sweet scent of roses as if the ethereal woman's essence accompanied him.

Another light flashed on the outskirts of the city, and with immortal speed Nikandros leaped to the cliff face below and then onto the sand where a young woman and a black jaguar stood as if waiting for him.

He stared at the ring on her finger, and the edges of his mouth lifted. "I am Nikandros," he said. "Sonja once told me that her daughter and I would be great friends."

The young woman smiled and walked to him. "Yes. I have seen that too. My name is Astridr." The jaguar padded over and rubbed her head against Nikandros. "Algiz likes you."

"Then trust her judgment," Nikandros said as he ran a hand over the feline's sleek coat. "There is a place—a school of sorts—where women are free to learn and teach. It is a safe place to begin your journey, and there are others like you, who have the gift of sight."

"Will you take me there?"

"Yes," Nikandros said with a nod. "And you are wel-come to stay in my home for as long as you wish. It is close to the school."

"And will you share with me the story of your life?"

"I am a warrior," he said and proceeded to guide her along the beach.

They walked up a set of steep steps carved from stone that led to an expansive terrace garnishing views of the ocean and parts of Salerno. Behind her, Astridr noted a stone villa built into the rock face with viewing platforms facing every direction.

"Is this your home?"

"Yes," Nikandros said. "Well, for as long as any immortal can live before the breadth of our lives raises questions." He motioned to a stone outcrop. They sat together and he began his story. "Perhaps it is strange, but even after so many years have come and gone, the memories of my life as a child are quite vivid. My father built boats in what was known as Mycenae…"

CHAPTER 17

REFLECTION

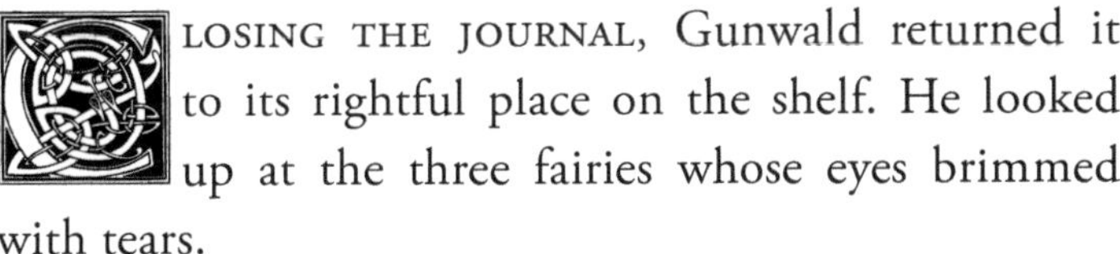

CLOSING THE JOURNAL, Gunwald returned it to its rightful place on the shelf. He looked up at the three fairies whose eyes brimmed with tears.

"Ladies, why do you insist on my rereading these journals when they always make you cry?"

Maeve sniffed and wiped her eyes with the tip of Kelda's peacock feather. "Because no matter how many times you tell us the story leading up to Astridr's birth, it is always with such heart, dear Gunwald, and also because we want you to continue—"

"—and we know you'll say no!" Kelda cut in, blushing even as she spoke the words.

Gunwald tilted his head and sighed. "Tomorrow eve… Once I have written Astridr's story as it plays out, I promise to read the next journal from long ago."

The instant expression of joy on Kelda's face made him smile. He turned and walked toward the waterfall, and as he did, his youthful appearance began to fade and silver hair framed his aged face. The flutter of wings and a sweet scent brought his attention to a hovering fairy.

"Gunwald," she said. "I have something for you." The scribe cupped his hands as the fairy emptied a handful of rose petals into his waiting palms. "The Lady sends her love and says she looks forward to hearing you read on the morrow."

"Selby, I…" Gunwald's need for words disappeared when he brought the roses to his nose and inhaled their intimate perfume.

"Keep writing," the fairies said in unison. "For after sadness, joy is often found."

"Yes," the scribe said. "Such is the way of stories."

ACKNOWLEDGEMENTS

Thanks to my beta readers, Jack Beverly, Suesie Shaw, and Jennifer Webster, for taking the time to read the manuscript in its earliest form; your helpful comments were much appreciated. To Anne Victory and the other ladies at Victory Editing, thank you!

To Becky Stonehouse, thank you for breathing life into my characters through your beautiful illustrations. You truly are a "Creative."

As always, thanks to Brian Beverly for your unconditional love, and for taking my words and music into your studio and producing *Hakon's Song*. And to my sons, Angus and Jack, thank you for your endless support and encouragement, and the enlightening conversations about historical events and characters.

And thanks to you, the readers, book bloggers, and reviewers who take the time to acknowledge my books. Your messages and reviews are appreciated.

ABOUT THE AUTHOR

Mandy Jackson-Beverly was born in Pyramid Hill, Victoria, Australia—population 419—and grew up around the rugged coastline and rolling hills of Tasmania. Upon moving to England, she discovered the tantalizing London fashion scene and fell in love with the concept of the creative collective. Later in Los Angeles, she found her own creative freedom among the thriving, no-holds-barred visionaries of the music video world.

Mandy has worked as a costume designer and stylist for an amazing array of creative dynamos including photographer Herb Ritts; directors Joel and Ethan Coen, David Fincher, and Julien Temple; and music icons David Bowie, Madonna, and Tina Turner. She taught art and theater in high schools, is a contributor to *The Huffington Post,* and reviews books for *The New York Journal of Books.* These days she lives with her family in Ojai, California, and spins stories for her readers' pleasure as well as her own.

When Mandy's not writing or reading (she has a fascination with Jung), she's cooking, painting, or on walkabout—preferably in Italy.

www.mandyjacksonbeverly.com.

Author of *A Secret Muse*, *The Devil And The Muse*, and *The Legend of Astridr: Birth*.

www.ingramcontent.com/pod-product-compliance
Lightning Source LLC
Chambersburg PA
CBHW041733300726
48981CB00020B/486/J